D0007117

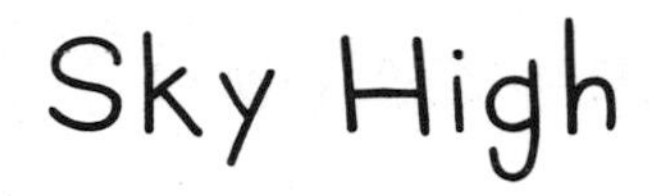
Sky High

ZIGZAG KIDS

OTHER BOOKS
IN THE ZIGZAG KIDS SERIES

Number One Kid

Big Whopper

Flying Feet

Star Time

Bears Beware

Super Surprise

PATRICIA REILLY GIFF

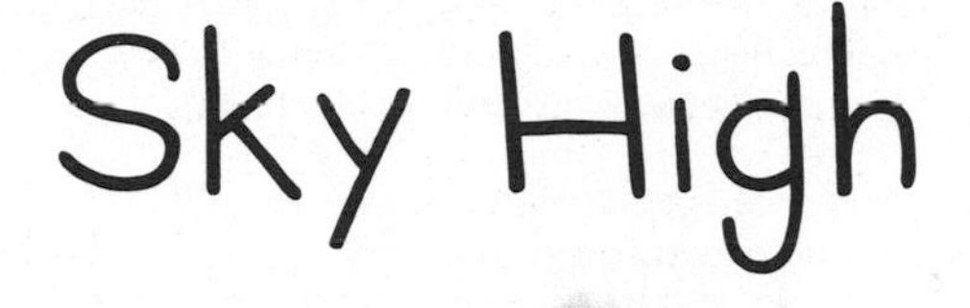

illustrated by

ALASDAIR BRIGHT

This is a work of fiction. Names, characters, places, and incidents either are the product of the author's imagination or are used fictitiously. Any resemblance to actual persons, living or dead, events, or locales is entirely coincidental.

 Published in the United States by Wendy Lamb Books, an imprint of Random House Children's Books, a division of Random House, Inc., New York.

Wendy Lamb Books and the colophon are trademarks of Random House, Inc.

Visit us on the Web! randomhouse.com/kids

Educators and librarians, for a variety of teaching tools, visit us at RHTeachersLibrarians.com

Library of Congress Cataloging-in-Publication Data
Giff, Patricia Reilly.
Sky high / by Patricia Reilly Giff ; illustrated by Alasdair Bright. — 1st ed.
p. cm. — (Zigzag kids)
ISBN 978-0-385-74274-0 (hardcover) — ISBN 978-0-375-99074-8 (lib. bdg.)
ISBN 978-0-307-97701-4 (pbk.) — ISBN 978-0-307-97702-1 (ebook)
[1. Inventors—Fiction.] I. Bright, Alasdair, ill. II. Title.
PZ7.G3626Sk 2012
[Fic]—dc23
2011049999

Printed in the United States of America
10 9 8 7 6 5 4 3 2 1
First Edition

Random House Children's Books supports the First Amendment and celebrates the right to read.

For Anne Reilly Eisele,
my sister,
with love

And with thanks to Barbara Perris,
copy chief, for her inspired care and
attention to my books all these years.
I'm truly grateful.
—P.R.G.

• • •

Special thanks to my great friend,
Jenny Goodes
—A.B.

Yolanda

Sumiko

Charlie

Destiny

Gina

Mitchell

Habib
Clifton
Trevor
Beebe
Angel
Peter

CHAPTER 1

FRIDAY

It was time for the Zigzag Afternoon Center. Charlie couldn't wait.

It was the first time for him this week. He'd been home sick with double earaches.

Borrrring!

Nana stayed home with him while Mom went to work. Nana vacuumed all day.

"Hoo-hoo," she said. "Borrrring!"

Nana wanted to be an inventor. Just like Charlie.

And that was the one thing good about being home. Charlie could invent all day.

He liked to invent all kinds of things.

But most of all, he wanted to invent something that would fly.

He'd look out at the clouds. He could almost see himself up there.

Sky-high!

Nana wanted to be sky-high, too. "Someday, we'll rocket ourselves right into space, Charlie," she said. "Hoo-hoo."

And right now he had two minutes to try his new invention: the Zinger-Winger.

On the way out to the school yard, he counted ceiling tiles. Maybe he could invent something with them.

He'd sit on one. There'd be a rocket underneath. *Zoom!*

Oof!

He bumped into someone. Someone he'd never seen before.

The man had a whoosh of tan hair.

It looked like a pigeon's nest.

"Counting ceiling tiles?" The man rubbed his elbow.

"It's for an invention," Charlie said. "I just don't know what yet."

"I count ceiling tiles, too," the man said. "I'm an inventor."

Charlie looked up at him. That whoosh of hair. A plaid tie with a gravy stain. Huge teeth, like a beaver's.

Charlie felt his own teeth. He was glad they were a decent size.

Charlie and the man walked along the hall together.

"I'm Mr. Redfern," said the man. "Everyone else has met me."

Charlie nodded. "I've been home sick." He rubbed his nose. He hoped he hadn't broken it when he bumped into Mr. Redfern.

"We're having an inventing fair at the Afternoon Center," Mr. Redfern said. "And not only that. There'll be something exciting. I call it a Great Happening!"

Mr. Redfern nodded. "I can't tell everyone about it yet." He grinned and showed his beaver teeth. "But believe me. It's exciting."

What could it be? Charlie wondered.

Mr. Redfern waved his arms around. His hair waved, too.

"I'll be here for a week," he said. "We'll set up a lab. We'll work on ideas! Projects all over the place!"

Mr. Redfern stopped short.

Charlie bumped into him again.

“What’s your name?” Mr. Redfern asked. He rubbed his other elbow.

“It’s Charlie.”

They reached the end of the hall.

Charlie started up the stairs. Mr. Redfern started down.

“Good to meet you, Chuck,” Mr. Redfern called after him.

"My name's Charlie."

But Mr. Redfern had disappeared.

"Things are looking up, Chuck," Charlie told himself. "The Zinger-Winger. An inventing fair. A Great Happening."

He thought about it. He'd try out the Zinger this afternoon. He'd work on it all week.

Right now, it had a few problems.

It didn't really fly straight.

It didn't really fly far.

But somehow, he'd change all that.

What an invention it would be.

Not quite a plane.

Not quite a rocket.

Charlie jumped up.

One of these days, he'd even touch the ceiling.

He headed out to the school yard.

"Hoo-hoo!" he yelled.

CHAPTER 2

STILL FRIDAY

Charlie spotted Mitchell at the door. "Hey," he called.

Mrs. Farelli, the toughest teacher at the Center, was right behind him. "Do I hear a hyena?" she asked.

Charlie ducked his head. "Come on outside," he whispered to Mitchell. "Watch my Zinger-Winger in action."

Mitchell looked back toward the lunchroom. "We have to hurry," he said. "It's almost time for snack."

They rushed out the door.

Outside it was warm and sunny.

Jake the Sweeper was growing a garden in one corner of the yard. The vegetables were half as tall as Charlie.

Rows of beans twirled on sticks.

Cabbages poked up their heads.

Clifton, a kindergarten kid, was crawling around in the tomatoes. He held up a jar.

"I'm getting bugs for the new science lab," he called.

"Want to watch my Zinger-Winger?" Charlie called back.

Clifton put the bottle down on a rock. "Sure."

Charlie looked around.

A couple of kids stood near him. Yolanda, the artist. Gina, who wanted to be an opera singer. Peter Petway, who wrote the Afternoon Center newspaper.

Wait until they saw the Zinger-Winger in action!

"Stand back," Charlie said. "Who knows what this thing will do?"

At home, he'd had the first trial run.

He'd jumped on the back of the couch.

He'd wound up.

"Go, Charlie!" Nana had yelled.

He'd thrown the Zinger.

Nana had ducked before it hit her in the head.

"Hoo-hoo!" she'd said.

Now Charlie gave the Zinger-Winger a pat.

Everything was in place. The paper cup nose. The paper clip propellers.

He held it up over his head.

He began to run . . .

. . . across the yard.

It was hard to see where he was going.

Uh-oh.

Through Jake's garden.

Into Clifton's bug jar.

"Oh, no!" Clifton yelled.

"Watch out for the tomatoes!" Mitchell shouted.

Charlie took a leap.

It was time to let go of the Zinger.

He threw it as hard as he could.

Up it went.

There was a zinger of a noise.

"Sky-high!" Charlie yelled.

The Zinger-Winger went straight into a tree.

It teetered on a branch.

"Oh, no!" Charlie said.

He felt something under one foot.

A squashed tomato.

Clifton was yelling. "My bugs escaped! They're crawling away as fast as their legs can carry them."

"And that's a lot of legs," Mitchell said.

Jake came outside. "That was my best tomato." He held his head.

Clifton looked as if he might cry. "I'll have to start over," he said. "I'll never be ready for the Great Happening."

"What went wrong?" Charlie whispered.

"Everything," Mitchell said.

"Sorry, Jake. Sorry, Clifton," Charlie said.

Peter Petway called over. "I'll write this up in the *Zigzag News—Read All About It*. 'Rocketplane crashes! Also bugs and tomatoes.'"

"Maybe it's snack time," Mitchell said.

"I'll come, too," Clifton said.

"I'm going to do something good for you," Charlie told Clifton.

"What?" Clifton asked.

"I don't know yet," Charlie said. "But something."

He went over to Jake. "I'll make up for the tomato," he said. "Somehow."

He looked at the tree.

The Zinger-Winger was too high to reach.

There went his invention.

He'd be the only inventor at the fair without an invention.

He walked backward into the school.

He was still looking at his poor Zinger-Winger.

The nose was dented.

One wing was on the ground.

The other was covered with leaves.

He went downstairs to the lunchroom.

What else could go wrong?

CHAPTER 3

STILL FRIDAY

Charlie was the last one in the lunchroom.

Mr. Redfern was up in front. He was standing on a box. "Don't forget next week is inventing week," he called.

"I used to be the bug guy," Clifton said.

"Pick a project," Mr. Redfern said. "Write about it on a poster."

"My poster will be better than my invention," Yolanda said.

Mr. Redfern was still talking. "Next Saturday, we'll invite the world to see our work."

"The whole world will see my Super-Fast Jump Rope," Sumiko said.

"Maybe just the neighborhood," Mr. Redfern said, and grinned.

"I'm making a Rainbow Gooper-Upper," Destiny said. "It will turn hair a million colors."

"I'll do a singing project," Gina said. *"La-la-de-la."*

"I'll do something with juggling." Habib frowned. "But I don't know what."

If only he hadn't ruined his Zinger-Winger, Charlie thought.

Mr. Redfern jumped off the box. "Don't forget about the Great Happening," he called.

He went out the door.

"Line up," said Destiny, the lunchroom helper.

Everyone raced to the front.

Today was carrot cupcake day.

"Hey, Charlie," Destiny said. "Too bad you were sick all week. But you're in luck. I have something for you."

"Hoo-hoo," Charlie said.

"Calm down, young man," the lunch lady said. She was stirring a bunch of tomatoes.

She was probably going to cook them into tomato soup with lumps.

Yuck.

Destiny pulled something out of a cabinet. She dusted it off with her sleeve.

She held it out to Charlie.

A leftover cheese popper from Monday!

Charlie turned it over in his hand.

It was round and tan.

It looked harder than Nana's homemade cookies.

It probably tasted just as strange.

"I know poppers are your favorite," Destiny said. "Better than cupcakes, right?"

"Thanks," Charlie told her. "You're the best."

No one would eat that popper in a million years.

Clifton walked over. He was shaking his

head. “I had all those ants,” he said through a mouthful of cupcake. “I had a beetle mother and father and two beetle kids.”

“How do you know they were a family?” Charlie asked.

Next to him, Mitchell was trying not to laugh.

But Charlie could see Clifton was ready to cry.

“Don’t worry,” Charlie said. “I’ll think of something to help.”

He tried not to breathe too hard. The whole room smelled like tomatoes.

Destiny was waiting.

Charlie took a bite out of the popper.

A small bite.

Yes, it was hard as a rock.

His tooth might even be broken.

“How does it taste?” Destiny asked.

“Good,” he told her.

Destiny smiled. She went to the front of the room.

She held out the tray of cupcakes to the line of kids.

Charlie's mouth watered for a cupcake. But he couldn't hurt Destiny's feelings.

Mitchell leaned over. "Careful. You don't want that popper to fall on your foot. You'll break your toes."

Charlie watched Mitchell eat.

He tried not to think about cupcakes. Instead, he thought about inventing.

He looked down at the popper. Maybe he could make it fly.

He'd call it the Amazing Popper-Upper.

There was a ruler in his backpack, and an apple left over from lunch.

He put the apple on the table.

He balanced the ruler on top of it.

"A seesaw," Mitchell said.

Charlie put the popper on one end of the ruler.

"Take cover!" Mitchell yelled. "Cheese popper blasting through!"

Charlie slammed the other end of the ruler with his fist.

The popper flew.

It didn't go very high.

And it came down fast.

Plunk!

Right into the pot of tomatoes.

Tomato mush flew all over the place. . . .

Onto the lunch lady's hat, which looked like a shower cap.

Onto the carrot cupcakes.

For a moment, no one made a sound.

Mitchell's mouth was wide open.

"That Charlie," Clifton said. "He lost my bug family. And now he's ruining the snacks."

The lunch lady beckoned to Charlie. "I think we should have a talk."

Charlie followed her into the kitchen.

He walked as slowly as he could.

Too bad he wasn't still home sick.

CHAPTER 4

MONDAY

Charlie started down the stairs.

He was on his way to the lunchroom.

He was in a zinger of trouble.

Friday, the lunch lady had put her hands on her hips.

Red polka-dots had covered her shirt.

"No more inventing for you, Charlie," she'd said.

"Forever?" he'd asked.

She'd looked up at the ceiling. "For at least a week."

A week!

"You might help out here," the lunch lady said. "I have no time to keep this place clean *and* invent new snacks."

"I guess so," Charlie had said.

"Start Monday," she'd said. "There's plenty to do."

Now it was Monday.

He hoped the lunch lady didn't want him to cook.

"Hey, Chip," said a voice behind him.

Charlie turned.

"I've been looking for you," Mr. Redfern said.

Charlie swallowed.

The Inventing Fair and the Great Happening would be over before he even began.

"Come down to the new lab," Mr. Redfern said. "You can see what's going on."

Charlie looked toward the lunchroom.

He shook his head.

"You can have snack anytime," Mr. Redfern said.

"I guess so," Charlie said.

They walked down the hall together.

Mr. Redfern threw open the door to the lab.

"Whew!" Charlie said.

Chairs were upside down.

Dust covered the tables.

Charlie sneezed about eight times.

Mr. Redfern sneezed, too. "What do you think, Chase?" he asked.

Some science lab! But Charlie didn't say that. "It's going to be . . . ," he began.

"Yes, stupendous." Mr. Redfern rubbed his hands together. "It takes imagination. We just have to add a lot of stuff."

Charlie nodded. It would take a lot of imagination to get this place going.

"A boy's collecting insects," Mr. Redfern said. "Someone's making a typhoon. And someone is flying a rocket all over the place."

Did he mean me? Charlie wondered.

"The Great Happening is going to be . . ." Mr. Redfern raised his shoulders. "Spectacular."

"What—" Charlie began.

Mr. Redfern rushed on. "Want to get this place set up with me?"

"I'm on my way to the lunchroom," Charlie said.

Mr. Redfern pulled a bag of pretzels out of his pocket.

"Don't worry," he said. "You won't starve to death, Calvin."

Mr. Redfern rolled up his long sleeves.

He began to push tables around.

Charlie didn't have sleeves to roll up. But he began to push tables, too.

Mitchell stuck his head in the door. "Is this the new lab?"

He looked as if he didn't believe it.

Charlie didn't believe it, either.

Now Mr. Redfern jumped on his desk.

He waved a mop over his head.

"Have to get rid of the cobwebs," he said.

Charlie and Mitchell put chairs around the tables.

"Looking better already," Mr. Redfern said.

Habib came in the door. "The lunch lady wants to see you both," he told Charlie and Mitchell.

Charlie gave the table one more push.

"See you tomorrow, Chris," Mr. Redfern said.

Charlie nodded.

He and Mitchell went down the hall.

"I'm in trouble, too," Mitchell said. "I was working on a typhoon thing. I spilled water all over the lunchroom."

A typhoon. What an idea!

"I have to help the lunch lady for a week," Mitchell said.

And now the lunch lady was standing in the doorway.

She went to the closet door. "Stand back!"

She opened it slowly.

A huge pile of junk clattered out.

"You two could clean this," she said. "Neaten up the whole thing."

It would be worse than cooking.

But then Ramón, the college helper, blew his whistle.

Afternoon Center was over for the day.

"See you tomorrow," the lunch lady said.

Charlie and Mitchell rushed upstairs and out the door.

Charlie made a list in his head.

Help with bugs.

Help with garden.

Help in lunchroom.

It was almost too much to think about.

CHAPTER 5

TUESDAY

Charlie slid along the walls.

He ducked behind doors.

He didn't want to see Mr. Redfern.

No, he didn't want Mr. Redfern to see him.

How could he tell Mr. Redfern that he couldn't invent?

He'd have to say he had to help the lunch lady.

"Hey, Charlie!" Clifton yelled. He was pushing a green box along in front of him. "I've been looking for you."

The box looked as if it was falling apart.
Charlie looked over his shoulder.
No Mr. Redfern.
Whew!
"Hi, Clifton," he said.

"Let's go outside," Clifton said. "We'll find my beetle family."

Charlie shook his head. "Sorry. I have to help the lunch lady."

Clifton looked down at the floor. "I was counting on you," he said.

"As soon as I can," Charlie said. "Really."

He went into the big kitchen.

Today the snack was applesauce.

Charlie couldn't think of anything worse.

Not unless it was tomato soup with a rock-hard popper on the bottom.

The lunch lady wore a striped shower cap. She pushed it back a little.

She pointed to the closet.

Charlie looked over her shoulder.

The closet was filled with empty cardboard tubes.

Boxes. Piles of plastic spoons. Wire. There was even an empty fish tank.

"Throw it all away," the lunch lady said.

That good stuff!

Mr. Redfern would love it.

Charlie and Mitchell piled everything up in their arms.

Charlie rested a carton on his head. It almost covered his eyes.

They zigzagged out of the kitchen.

They headed down the hall.

"Toot-toot!" Mitchell yelled.

Outside, they headed for Jake's huge litter bin.

“Hey,” Mitchell said. “What’s that?”

Charlie pushed the carton up so he could see. “Sneakers!” he said. “Hanging out of the litter bin.”

The sneakers belonged to Mr. Redfern.

He popped out of the bin. “Hey, Kenneth,” he said to Charlie. “And Michael. I’ve been looking for inventing material.”

Charlie pulled the carton off his head.

Mr. Redfern’s eyes widened. He clicked his

beaver teeth. "Look at all that! It's just what we need."

He gave Charlie a pat on the shoulder.

"You two have saved the day. Let's go back inside."

They followed Mr. Redfern through the door.

"What will the lunch lady say?" Charlie whispered.

"She'll just be glad to be rid of this junk," Mitchell said.

They all went down to the lab.

There was no dust today.

The tables were lined up neatly.

Charlie dumped everything on the floor. Balls of twine rolled across the tile.

Spoons clattered.

"Stupendous!" Mr. Redfern glanced toward the door. "Come and see what's going on," he told someone.

Charlie looked toward the door, too.

It was the lunch lady. Her mouth opened.

Charlie held his breath.

She winked. "Good work, boys," she said.

CHAPTER 6
WEDNESDAY

Charlie watered the lunch lady's plants.

There were a million of them.

A stem with two little leaves had fallen off the smallest one.

Maybe he should throw it out.

But it was dying of thirst.

He stuck it in a plastic cup. He gave it a drink.

Plant watering took a lot of time.

Someday he'd invent a . . .

He stopped to think.

A pipe with a bunch of arms! They'd go from the sink to the plants.

You'd turn on the water and . . .

He'd call it the Sink-to-Drink.

Next to him, Mitchell was shining an apple on his shirt. "Talking to yourself, Charlie?" he asked.

"A week without inventing is a long time," Charlie said.

And now he had to hurry.

Clifton was waiting.

So was Mr. Redfern.

And what about helping Jake in the garden?

There was just too much to think about. The Zigzag Afternoon Center was getting harder than school.

"All right, Charlie," the lunch lady said at last. "You can go now."

Charlie went to the lunchroom door.

He looked both ways.

Mr. Redfern wasn't in the hall.

But Clifton was. He was carrying that huge green box.

They went out to Jake's garden.

Charlie tried not to look at the stepped-on vegetables.

He stayed away from a bent-over tomato plant.

"How about we look for bugs on the other side of the school yard?" he asked Clifton.

"That wouldn't work," Clifton said.

"Sure it would," Charlie said. "The earth is nice and soft from last night's rain."

"Do you see how far away that is?"

Charlie squinted. "About fourteen steps."

Clifton slapped the box. "Do you think my bug family could walk that far?"

Charlie tried not to laugh. "How can you tell one bug family from another?"

Clifton didn't answer. He began to dig near the tomato plant.

He dug with a spoon.

Charlie watched. He thought about being able to tell one bug from another.

Suppose he watched bugs all day?

He'd draw their heads, their skinny legs, their stomachs.

He'd put their names beside their pictures.

Ant. Bee. Spider.

He'd make a book. He'd call it the Bug-Looker-Upper.

Most of all, he'd draw the bugs that had wings.

Bees and darning needles. Butterflies.

He'd figure out how they could fly.

He looked up at the tree. If only he could fly his Zinger-Winger.

"There's another spoon in the box," Clifton said.

Charlie began to dig, too. "How about a worm?" he asked.

Clifton sat back. "A worm isn't a bug."

Charlie nodded. He lifted a couple of ants on the spoon.

He put them in the box with a scoop of dirt.

Poor ants.

Would they be stuck in that box forever? It was no place for ants. Falling apart. Damp from rain.

Still, he spooned in a few more.

"Nice," Clifton said. "You're keeping the family together."

Charlie could see the lunch lady in lunch-room window.

And Mr. Redfern was looking out the lab window.

The ants were going crazy. They ran from one side of the box to the other.

Mr. Redfern opened his window.

"There you are, Cooper," Mr. Redfern called.

At the same time, Clifton said, "Here's a beetle family." He piled them in the box with the ants.

"We're coming!" Charlie called to Mr. Redfern.

Clifton jammed the lid on the box.

They walked back into the center. They left dirt trails behind them.

Charlie swallowed. He still hadn't told Mr. Redfern about not inventing anything the whole week.

How had all this happened?

CHAPTER 7

STILL WEDNESDAY

Charlie blinked.

The lab looked different.

Mr. Redfern's jacket was spattered with paint.

One wall was yellow.

Another was purple with white clouds.

Yolanda stood on a bench.

She was covered with paint, too.

"Hey, Charlie," she said. "What do you think of this?"

He looked at the wall.

What was it?

He had no idea.

"Neat," he said.

"It's going to be a rocket ship," Mr. Redfern said. "Aimed for the planet Commodore."

"I've never heard of that planet," Charlie said.

"Me neither," Mr. Redfern said. "But you never know."

The lunch lady's closet stuff covered two tables.

Charlie ran his hand over everything.

He could think of a dozen things to invent.

Too bad.

It was too late.

Mr. Redfern waved at the chairs. He sat down on an orange one.

Charlie sat on a red one.

"Watch out for my family," Clifton said. "I'm going to get a snack."

Charlie took a breath.

It was time to tell Mr. Redfern he couldn't invent.

Not one thing.

Not even for the Great Happening.

But Mr. Redfern spoke first. "Do you think of inventing things all day?"

Charlie nodded.

Mr. Redfern grinned. "You're a true inventor, Christopher."

Charlie nodded a little.

Then he began.

"I squashed Jake's tomatoes. My Zinger-Winger crashed in a tree."

He shook his head. "My Popper-Upper blasted in the lunch lady's soup."

"Tomato soup with lumps?" Mr. Redfern said.

Was Mr. Redfern trying not to laugh?

Charlie nodded. "I guess the Popper-Upper went out with the soup," he said.

Mr. Redfern ran a hand through his pigeon's-nest hair. "I know exactly what we'll do," he said.

Charlie opened his mouth again.

He still hadn't told Mr. Redfern about the lunch lady and no inventing for almost a week.

But then he heard Ramón's whistle.

Afternoon Center was over for the day.

"I can't invent," he said in a rush. "The lunch lady said so."

He didn't wait to hear what Mr. Redfern would say.

He dashed toward the door.

Ramón blew his whistle again.

Charlie headed for the bus.

Whew! He was glad the day was over.

CHAPTER 8

THURSDAY

"Have a tomato," the lunch lady said. "From Jake's garden."

Charlie took one in his hand.

It was warm from the sun.

"Jake loves to grow vegetables," she said. "I love to cook."

Charlie had almost forgotten.

He had to help Jake.

He had to make up for the Zinger-Winger crash.

And what about the bugs?

He wondered where they had gone.

He had to do something about them, too.

He'd do that as soon as . . .

As soon as he helped the lunch lady.

She was standing there munching on a tomato.

Charlie leaned forward. "I really miss inventing."

"I want to talk to you about that," the lunch lady said.

Would she say no inventing for another week?

For a year?

Or maybe not until he was an old man with beaver teeth and pigeon's-nest hair.

"Hey, what's that?" She pointed to the window.

Mr. Redfern was dragging a ladder across the yard.

Charlie couldn't believe it. "He's going for my Zinger-Winger."

"He called it Kevin's Zinger-Winger." The lunch lady grinned. "He said it was a great idea. It just needed a little help."

She raised her shoulders. "He thinks that someday a rocket like that might fly to . . ."

She looked as if she was trying to remember. "The planet . . ."

"Commodore?" Charlie said.

The lunch lady nodded. "I've never heard of that planet."

"You never know," Charlie said in a Mr. Redfern voice.

Now Mr. Redfern shoved the ladder against the tree.

"That ladder looks rickety," the lunch lady said.

"Maybe I should help," Charlie said.

"Maybe you should," she said.

Charlie went toward the door.

"I think it's time for you to invent again," the lunch lady said. "You've helped me. And Mr. Redfern thinks you're ready for big ideas."

"Thanks," Charlie said.

He raced down the hall.

He jumped up toward the ceiling tiles.

He could invent again!

There wasn't much time until the inventing fair.

But maybe . . .

"Slow down, Kevin!" the lunch lady called after him, and laughed.

"Hoo-hoo!" Charlie said.

He passed the art room. A bunch of kids were helping Mrs. Farelli make posters.

Destiny was drawing a poster. It was of a girl with lots of hair. The poster was for her Rainbow Gooper-Upper.

"I'm coming!" Charlie yelled to Mr. Redfern.

Mr. Redfern couldn't have heard him.

He was climbing.

One step.

Two steps.

The ladder shook.

Mr. Redfern shook.

"Watch out!" Charlie cried.

Too late.

Oof!

Mr. Redfern hit the ground.

Charlie stood over him. "Are you all right?"

"That's the thing with inventions, Caleb," Mr. Redfern said. "Sometimes things don't work out exactly right."

Above him, Charlie could see the Zinger-Winger.

"Maybe I could climb up," Charlie said.

Mr. Redfern scrambled to his feet.

He looked a little worried.

"I'll hold the ladder," he said.

Charlie took a step up.

Even though Mr. Redfern was holding the ladder, it wiggled.

It shook.

Charlie took four more steps.

The Zinger-Winger was just over his head.

He squinted at the blue sky.

He saw the clouds and a daytime moon.

Someday he'd be sky-high.

He knew it.

He reached for the Zinger-Winger.

Just one more step!

But he'd reached the top of the ladder.

"Go for it!" Mr. Redfern said.

Charlie lunged.

And there it was in his hand.

But he felt himself going backward.

Oof!

He and the Zinger-Winger landed on the ground.

"Good work!" Mr. Redfern said. "Never let a good invention go to waste."

CHAPTER 9

FRIDAY

Charlie yawned. He'd been up late last night.

He'd tried to do everything.

Draw posters.

Paint wings.

Fill a bag with dirt. With seeds. With pieces of his father's pipe.

Pile sticks up from the garage. Find bells and string.

But right now it was time for the Afternoon Center.

He had to hurry.

He went out to Jake's garden.

He brought the sticks, and the string, and the bells.

He pounded everything in.

It was a crooked fence.

The string sagged.

But the bells would ring if someone stepped in the garden.

It was safe now.

No more squashed tomatoes.

Next Charlie headed for the lunchroom. He had just enough time for snack.

"It's from Jake's garden," the lunch lady said through a mouthful of salad.

Charlie took a cup of salad, too.

It was green.

Crunchy.

"It's my new invention," the lunch lady said. "Just Plain Cabbage."

"Neat," Charlie said.

He headed for the lab.

It was crowded with kids.

Tomorrow was the fair and the Great Happening.

On Saturday!

Peter Petway was working on the *Zigzag News—Read All About It.*

"It's my sloppy copy," Peter said. "But it's going to be the best one yet."

Charlie looked around.

Mitchell was stirring a pot of water. He was stirring fast.

Water slopped over the table, the floor, and Mitchell's shirt.

"It's my typhoon." Mitchell wiped a drop off his chin. "When I stop stirring, it'll keep going. At least, I hope so."

"Hoo-hoo!" Charlie said.

He watched Yolanda pour paints from one jar to another.

She looked up. "I'm trying to see what happens when I mix colors together."

"They're mixing together on the floor with Mitchell's typhoon," Charlie said.

"It looks like my Rainbow Gooper-Upper," Destiny said.

"Good work," Mr. Redfern said.

Yolanda's wall painting was covered with cloth. "I'll show it tomorrow," she said.

"I can't find my bugs," Clifton said. "I've looked all over the room."

"I'll help find them," Charlie said.

He went out to the hall with Clifton.

They crawled along the floor.

It was a little dusty.

"Hey," Clifton said. "Here's the beetle father hiding in the corner. And the beetle mother."

Charlie scurried after some ants.

He and Clifton took the bugs back into the lab.

Charlie set up the lunch lady's fish tank.

He added dirt.

And leaves.

He put in a pipe for a bug tunnel.

"Neat," Clifton said.

But now Charlie was looking around for the Zinger-Winger.

He found it on Mr. Redfern's desk.

He tied on the new wings he'd painted last night.

Mr. Redfern watched over his shoulder. "Go ahead, Conrad. Let it fly," he said.

Charlie wound up the Zinger-Winger.

He twirled it over his head.

He twirled until he was dizzy.

"Duck, everyone!" Mitchell called.

Clifton crawled under the desk.

Mr. Redfern backed up against the window.

Beebe and Angel hid in the closet.

"Here we go," Mr. Redfern called. "Off to the planet Commodore!"

Charlie let go.

The Zinger-Winger zinged across the room. . . .

It didn't go high.

But it went fast.
The new wings were better than the old ones.
"Hoo-hoo!" Charlie yelled.
It shot straight toward the door.
At the same moment, the door opened.
A man stood there.
Oh, no.
The man tried to jump out of the way.
Too late.
The Zinger-Winger landed on his head.

The man grinned.

Charlie closed his eyes.

How did he know that man?

Had he seen him before?

"Come back tomorrow," Mr. Redfern told the man. "You're a day early for the Great Happening."

CHAPTER 10

SATURDAY

Today was the day!

Charlie was early.

He slid into the lab.

Mr. Redfern was there, too. "You'll be surprised at the Great Happening," he said.

Near the sink was the stem Charlie had saved. He gave it a little water.

"Too bad," he told Mr. Redfern. "My Sink-to-Drink isn't ready yet."

"That's the best thing about inventing," Mr. Redfern said. "There's always something to look forward to."

Now the room was filling with kids.

Parents came, too.

Nana was wearing her pilot boots.

The lunch lady bustled into the lab. She was carrying a tray filled with cups.

"Try one," she told Charlie.

He reached for a cup. There were raisins, he could see that, and Rice Krispies.

What else?

He took a taste.

"It's my secret snack invention," the lunch lady told him.

"Call it the Sweeter-Treater," Charlie said.

Everyone walked around the room.

Charlie could hear them crunching on the snack.

"It's a terrific fair," everyone was saying.

They all wanted to see Habib's juggling machine.

"It doesn't really juggle yet," Habib said. "I'm still working on it."

"That's what inventing is all about," said Mr. Redfern.

The door opened again.

And there he was. The man from yesterday.

"Here comes the Great Happening," Mr. Redfern said.

The man smiled with beaver teeth.

He looked like Mr. Redfern.

"It's my son, the former astronaut," Mr. Redfern said. He waved his arms around.

"My name is Jackson," the man said. "Sometimes my father calls me James. Or Jonathan. Or even Jimbo."

Mr. Redfern smiled, too. "He works at the science museum."

"I have to pick an inventor for next weekend," Jackson said. "It's Kids' Time at the museum."

He looked around. "Who should it be?"

Charlie thought.

Maybe it would be Habib, with his juggling machine.

Or Destiny, with her Gooper-Upper.

Maybe it would be

Mitchell. Even though his typhoon didn't have any waves.

Charlie swallowed.

That kid would be the luckiest kid in the world.

He knew it wouldn't be him.

He looked up.

Everyone was pointing.

Jake pointed out the window. "Charlie made a Stringer-Ringer for my garden."

"Don't forget the Bug Bedroom," Clifton called, pointing to the fish tank.

"Wait," Yolanda said.

She pulled the cloth off her painting.

"Stupendous!" Mr. Redfern said.

"Wow," Charlie said.

It was a painting of the Zinger-Winger . . . heading sky-high.

Jackson Redfern was looking at the real Zinger-Winger.

Mr. Redfern had hung it from the ceiling.

"Neat." Jackson Redfern nodded. "What do you say?" he asked everyone.

Charlie could see they were pointing at him now.

"A Stringer-Ringer, a Bug Bedroom, and most of all, the Zinger-Winger," Jackson said.

"That's an inventor," said Mr. Redfern.

"Read all about it in the *Zigzag News,*" Peter Petway said. "Charlie the inventor goes to the science museum."

And Nana said, "Reach for the sky, Charlie."

It was the best thing that had ever happened to him.

"Hoo-hoo!" he said.

PATRICIA REILLY GIFF is the author of many beloved books for children, including the Kids of the Polk Street School books, the Friends and Amigos books, and the Polka Dot Private Eye books. Several of her novels for older readers have been chosen as ALA-ALSC Notable Books and ALA-YALSA Best Books for Young Adults. They include *The Gift of the Pirate Queen; All the Way Home; Water Street; Nory Ryan's Song,* a Society of Children's Book Writers and Illustrators Golden Kite Honor Book for Fiction; and the Newbery Honor Books *Lily's Crossing* and *Pictures of Hollis Woods. Lily's Crossing* was also chosen as a *Boston Globe–Horn Book* Honor Book. Her most recent books are *R My Name Is Rachel, Storyteller,* and *Wild Girl,* as well as the first six books in the ZigZag Kids series. Patricia Reilly Giff lives in Connecticut.

Patricia Reilly Giff is available for select readings and lectures. To inquire about a possible appearance, please contact the Random House Speakers Bureau at rhspeakers@randomhouse.com.

ALASDAIR BRIGHT is a freelance illustrator who has worked on numerous books and advertising projects. He loves drawing and is never without his sketchbook. He lives in Bedford, England.